Leon's Fancy Dress Day

Alan MacDonald

Illustrated by Sally Anne Lambert

MACDONALD YOUNG BOOKS

Miss Trotter had news for her class. It
was the school fair on Saturday.
"There will be a fancy dress parade,"
she said. "You can all dress up. The
best costumes will win a prize."
The class all began to talk at once.

Leon's friends were excited. They were all going to enter the fancy dress parade. Only Leon looked worried.
"I'm going as a pirate," said Guy.
"And I'm going as a spaceman," said Felix.

"I've got my own doctors's outfit,"
said Patsy proudly. "What are you
going as, Leon?"
Leon looked at the ground.
"Er... um... it's a secret," he mumbled.

7

Leon didn't say a word on the
way home.
He was thinking about
the fancy dress
parade.

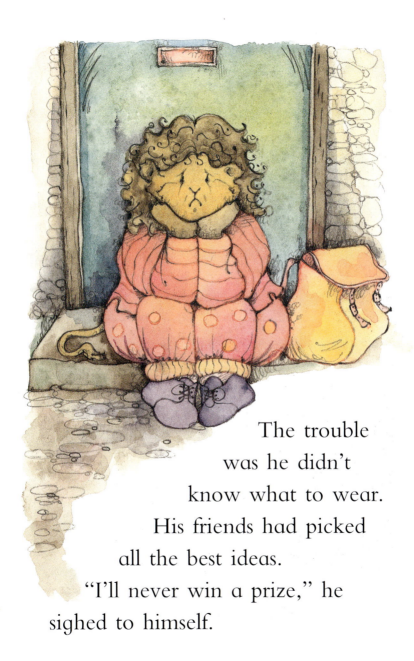

The trouble
was he didn't
know what to wear.
His friends had picked
all the best ideas.
"I'll never win a prize," he
sighed to himself.

9

At supper he told his mum about the parade.

"What can I go as?" asked Leon.

"All my friends are going to enter."

Leon's mum thought hard.

"There's your sister's ballet dress
upstairs. You could go as a good fairy,"
she said.

Leon made a face. He didn't want to
go as a good fairy. His friends would
laugh at him.

Leon looked in his mum and dad's
wardrobe.
He wanted to dress up as a cowboy.
But his mum's hat was too floppy.
And his dad's trousers were too big.

12

He tried to dress up as a clown.
But he used too much of his mum's
make-up.

He thought he might go as a ghost.
But he kept getting tangled up in the
sheet.
"I'll never win a prize," moaned
Leon.

14

Just then he saw something in his toy box.

It was a black mask. He'd cut it out of a cornflakes packet a long time ago.

GRRR...

Leon put it on and looked in the mirror. It looked good.

"I'm a big bad robber," growled Leon.

Leon's mum was watering the flowers.
Suddenly Leon jumped out at her.
"BOO!" he shouted.

"Hello Leon," smiled his mum.
"I'm a big bad robber," said Leon.
"Did I scare you?"
His mum just laughed.

Leon went off in a sulk. His mask was meant to be scary not funny.

He tripped over the garden hose.

"Ow! Stupid mask! I can't see where I'm going!"

On Saturday it was the summer fair.
Leon wore his big bad robber's mask.
It was the only costume he had.

19

All his friends were at the fair. Their
costumes were much better than
Leon's.
"I'll never win a prize,"
sighed Leon.

Leon saw Patsy standing on her own.
He wanted to jump out and scare her.
"BOO!" he shouted. But Patsy's
doctor's bag was on the ground.
Leon tripped over it and
fell flat on his
face.

21

"Are you all right, Leon?" asked
Patsy.
Leon groaned and rubbed his head.
He felt dizzy.

Doctor Patsy opened her bag.
"Where does it hurt?" she asked.
"All over," moaned Leon.

It was lucky Patsy had lots of
bandages with her.
She used them all up.

"I can't move. What have you done to
me?" moaned Leon.
"You said it hurt all over," replied
Patsy.

25

Just then Miss Trotter stood up. She
clapped her hands.
"The fancy dress parade is about to
start!"

Patsy helped Leon to stand up. She led
him over to join the line.

Miss Trotter was the judge. She looked
at all the costumes.
There were lots of good ones. But
when she got to Leon she stopped.

28

"Is that you in there, Leon? What a
clever idea to come as a mummy.
You really do look scary!"

Leon won first prize for his fancy dress costume. The prize was a big box of chocolates. He showed them proudly to his friends.

"But how am I going to eat them?" he asked.

"Never mind," laughed Patsy. "We'll help you, Leon!"

Look out for more fun titles in the First Storybook series.

Leon's Gets A Scarecut *by Alan MacDonald*

Leon must get his mane cut for Patsy's party. On the way to Sid's Barber Shop he meets some friends. Strangely they are all wearing new hats. Leon is a little nervous as Sid's new electric trimmer buzzes in his ears. He closes his eyes until it's over. Then he looks in the mirror. Help! He can't go to Patsy's party with a scarecut-haircut.

Mulberry Home Alone *by Sally Grindley*

Mulberry the dog doesn't like being home alone. But he tries to make the best of it. First he searches for his doggy crunchy things. Whoops! He's knocked over the rubbish bin. Then he decides to chase Cat. Whoops! He's crashed into the telephone table. Luckily, Mulberry isn't home alone for long.

Mulberry Alone in the Park *by Sally Grindley*

The front door has been left open. It must be doggy walkies time for Mulberry. So off he trots to the park. He has great fun chasing squirrels and doggy-paddling after the ducks. But then it starts to get dark. Mulberry is woken by a loud bang, then another. Bright colours light up the sky. Maybe being alone in the park is not such fun after all...

All these books and many more in the Storybook series can be purchased from your local bookseller. For more information about Storybooks, write to: *The Sales Department, Macdonald Young Books, 61 Western Road, Hove, East Sussex BN3 1JD.*